For Mum
and for Effi

First published 2017 by Walker Books Ltd, 87 Vauxhall Walk, London SE11 5HJ

2 4 6 8 10 9 7 5 3 1

© 2017 Daisy Hirst

The right of Daisy Hirst to be identified as author and illustrator of this work has been asserted
by her in accordance with the Copyright, Designs and Patents Act 1988

This book has been typeset in Stemple Schneider

Printed in China

British Library Cataloguing in Publication Data: a catalogue record for this book is available from the British Library

ISBN 978-1-4063-6331-9

www.walker.co.uk

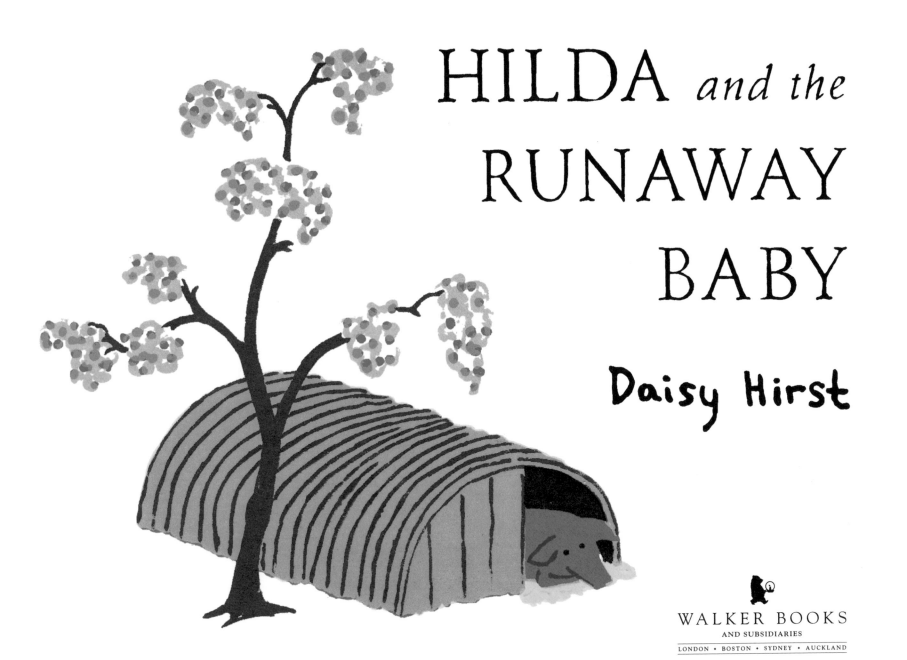

HILDA *and the* RUNAWAY BABY

Daisy Hirst

WALKER BOOKS
AND SUBSIDIARIES
LONDON · BOSTON · SYDNEY · AUCKLAND

Hilda lived in a small tin
house at the foot of a hill.
She had a trough, a bucket and an almond tree.
Sometimes she tried talking to them,
but even the almond tree
didn't say anything back.

I think I ought to be happy,
thought Hilda. *Life is peaceful.*
Nobody bothers me. I am always
where I expect myself to be.

At the top of the hill was a village, and in the village lived a baby, who was never where people expected him to be.

Which is why he was known

as the Runaway Baby.

He usually turned up somewhere,
but it worried his mum and dad.

When they went out for a walk, everyone
wanted to talk to the Runaway Baby's mum and dad.

The Runaway Baby did not talk.

But he did notice the cat on the dustbin,

yellow roses and a bird …

that was flying away.

Hilda had never seen a baby go so fast.

She realized the Runaway Baby could not stop the pram!

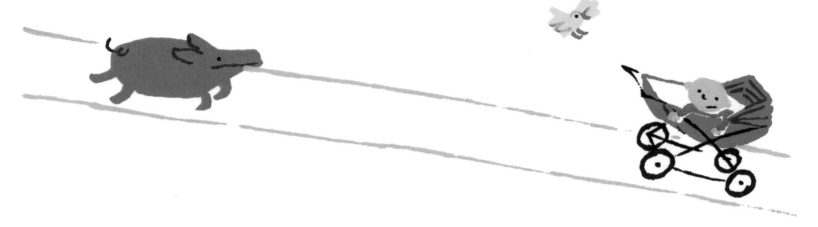

Hilda ran and ran, the pram raced on and on,

the Runaway Baby stretched, Hilda leapt …

and they fell in a heap in the sun.

"Hello, Baby," said Hilda. "My name is Hilda."

"Da," said the baby back.

"Yes," said Hilda, "that's right. And now
I think we'd better get you home."

"I've never been so tired in all my life," said Hilda. "A pig is not designed to stand up straight and push a pram."

"Da," said the Runaway Baby, and gave Hilda some of his milk and part of a broken biscuit he found in the pram.

Then the baby had an idea.

Pulling the pram was easier for Hilda, but they still had a long way to go. As they passed Hilda's tin house and her almond tree, the Runaway Baby fell asleep.

At last they came to the Runaway Baby's house. Hilda rang the doorbell and hid. The baby's mum and dad were very, very happy that he had come home.

When Hilda got back to her own house, it seemed a bit lonely and cold. She was exhausted, so she went straight to bed.

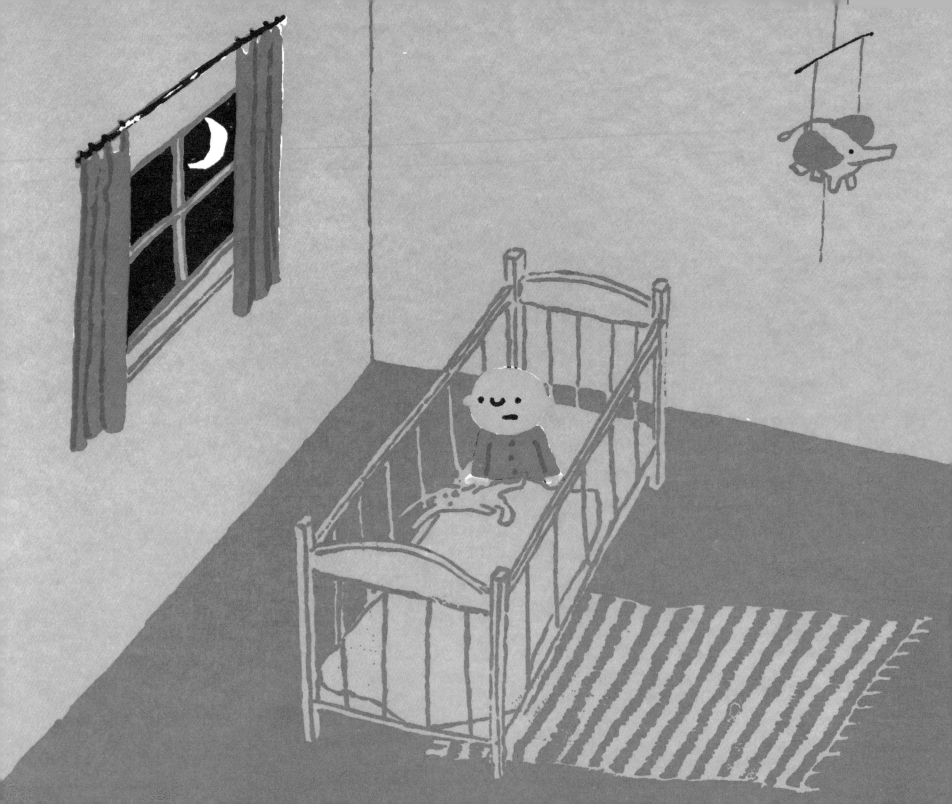

The Runaway Baby woke up in the night

and remembered Hilda …

and HOWLED.

Nothing seemed to comfort the Runaway Baby.

Down in the valley, Hilda heard the baby howl and was surprised to find herself leaving her house again, and setting off back up the hill.

Suddenly, the howling stopped.

"Hello, Baby," said Hilda.

"Da!" said the baby back.

The baby's mum and
dad let Hilda in, and
they all went to sleep.

Hilda never expected to end up here, but she and the
Runaway Baby soon found they had plenty to talk about.

And although the Runaway Baby still

turns up in surprising places ...

Hilda is always happy to find herself
where the baby expects her to be.